TEENAGE MUTANT TURTLES

ENTER: THE RAT KING

Written by Maureen Spurgeon
Illustrated by Clic Publishing

THE FOUR Teenage Mutant Hero Turtles never thought of Master Splinter as a half-human rat. He was just their friend. Once he had been the brilliant martial arts Professor Yoshi - the man that the evil Shredder from Dimension X, in the guise of a rival named Saki, had forced to flee in disgrace from Japan to America.

Penniless, Yoshi lived with the rats in a sewer. The same sewer where four unwanted turtles were dumped, and where a canister of radioactive mutagen goo had been emptied. This was a powerful substance that combined the characteristics and appearance of all who came into contact with it.

That's how the four turtles became mutant - half-turtle, half-teenager. And the wise and learned Professor Yoshi? His rat-like features were now as much part of him as his deep-sounding voice. Only the sewer rats stayed the same, with their long, hairy ears and whiskers, and their sharp claws and teeth.

Burne Thompson from television's Channel Six News hated rats - especially when they got into his car! "Scat!" he yelled, aiming a slap at an intruding rodent and swerving. "Beat it!"

His words were drowned by an ear-splitting crash. Steam hissed from a broken radiator. Burne gave a loud groan. Just his luck to plough into the back of a police car!

By the time he reached the Channel Six building where he was news editor, Burne had seen rats eating left-overs from dustbins, rats in empty tins, in fact, rats all over town.

He banged open the door to the news room. Everyone looked round at his torn clothes and the bandage on his forehead as he stormed towards news girl April O'Neil.

"You're going to dig up the facts about our city's rat problem! That's tonight's lead story!" he shouted.

For once, the Teenage Mutant Hero Turtles weren't too fond of the furry little creatures, either - not after Michaelangelo went to fetch the last box of pizza mix in the cupboard and found a rat had got there first!

"Hey, fur-face!" he yelled. What do you…?"

He got no further. The rat shook itself like a dog and covered Michaelangelo in flour!

"Yaachoooo!" The force of his sneeze sent the unwelcome visitor scurrying behind the dishes.

"I'll get him!" cried Donatello, lunging.

CRASH! The crockery flew, but the rat got clean away!

"Don't let him escape!" shouted Leonardo, diving - at exactly the same time as Raphael!

"Oooof!" **"Oooww!"**

By the time the rat had gone, the Turtles' lair looked like a war zone.

"Your reflexes must be dull, indeed," Splinter pronounced, "if a mere rodent can outwit you!"

"That furry little dude was more than mere!" Michaelangelo protested, but Leonardo waved a flipper at him.

"Sssh! Someone's coming!"

"Maybe the rat's back!" breathed Donatello.

"Tubuloso!" hissed Michaelangelo. "This time, we'll nail him!"

Nobody quite knew whether to be pleased or disappointed to see it was April!

"Uh, sorry, April," muttered Donatello, rather sheepishly. "We mistook you for a low-down, pizza-stealing rat!"

"I've been researching a story on rats!" April informed them. "I came to investigate the situation in the sewers, first hand!"

A strange expression suddenly appeared on Splinter's face. "Are you okay?" cried Leonardo.

"Yes…" faltered Splinter, waving a feeble paw. "Do not worry. It will pass…"

"Well, I'd better hustle!" April cut in, eyeing her watch. "I'm on the air in twenty minutes!"

It seemed like a lifetime to Irma, waiting for April in the Channel Six news van. Whether it was the heavy rain, or the low, black sky, she didn't know, but she seemed to see dozens of beady red eyes glaring at her. And she could hear chomping - like hundreds of teeth nibbling at hard rubber...

"Okay, Irma. Let's roll!" said April, climbing in beside her. She switched on the ignition.

There was a series of loud thumps as the van rocked and shook, then stopped altogether.

"Oh, no!" groaned Irma. "Two flat tyres!"

"Four flat tyres!" corrected April. "Irma, if I miss that broadcast, Burne will dock my pay!"

There was only one thing to do - get out and walk! Both girls kept their collars bunched up tight against the rain which swept across the deserted streets. Suddenly April grabbed Irma..

Could that pattering sound be raindrops? Or, was it...

"Rats!" April screamed at the claws and long tails appearing out of the drains. "Zillions and zillions of rats!"

"Let's get a cab!" cried Irma. "Taxi! Yoohoo!"

Four wheels screeched to a stop. Too bad the cab driver had also seen all those eyes!

"S-sorry!" he blustered, his foot hovering nervously over the accelerator. "No more than five passengers allowed!" The cab roared away, splashing Irma and April from head to foot. If a bus hadn't come along, they would have been surrounded by an army of rats.

Not that any of this would have bothered Burne Thompson, safe and dry in the Channel Six building! All that concerned him was getting the news bulletin out on time!

"Where's April O'Neil?" he thundered. "She's on in two minutes!"

"Okay, Burne!" cried April, almost falling through the door. "I'm ready!"

"This had better be good!" growled Burne - but April was already at the news desk.

"Good evening!" The Teenage Mutant Hero Turtles, watching April on their television, wondered why she looked so drawn and tense. "I hope this doesn't upset our viewers - but our city is being over-run by rats!" What she and Irma had seen made her shudder. "Horrible, disgusting creatures! Something must be done about these vicious rodents!"

Unknown to the Turtles and April, something was going on in the dimly-lit basement of Channel Six News. A strange, half-human shadow moved along the wall, and its long arm reached for a switch...

Next minute, millions of television screens went blank, including the Turtles' own!

"Hey!" yelled Michaelangelo. "Like, who pulled the plug?"

Before anyone could answer, the studio lights went back on.

"What happened to April?" Burne demanded, appearing on-screen and goggling at her empty chair. "She - she's gone!"

The Teenage Mutant Hero Turtles gulped. "April? Gone?"

Within minutes, the Turtle Van had arrived at the the Channel Six building and they leapt out, all twirling ropes with grappling hooks at one end.

"Okay!" yelled Leonardo. "All together!"

Four hooks were flung up the side of the building and the Turtles swiftly scaled the wall.

"Check it out!" ordered Michaelangelo, nodding frantically at a lighted window. "There's the studio she disappeared from!"

"Whoever heard of losing a commentator in the middle of a broadcast?" came Burne Thompson's angry voice. "Someone find April O'Neil!"

Burne didn't notice he was about to lose another member of his team! Two powerful, green arms reached from behind and pulled Irma into April's dressing room.

"The Turtles!" she gasped, delighted. She had always wanted to meet them!

"Quick, Irma!" rapped Leonardo. "What happened to April?"

Irma shrugged. "You know as much as I do! If you ask me it's those rats who chased us."

"But if April needed us," Michaelangelo cut in, "she'd call us on her Turtle-Com!"

"You mean," said Raphael, pointing a flipper towards her dressing table, "that Turtle-Com?"

Leonardo let out a deep breath. "Fellas," he said, "we've got to check every storm drain and sewer pipe in the city, until we find her!"

And with cries of *"Turtle powerrrrr!!!"* they swung out of the window and slid down the ropes to the ground.

Even with Master Splinter to help in their underground search, there was no sign of April. Leonardo began to wonder how long they could all carry on, especially Splinter. He had never seen such a glazed look in the Master's bright eyes, and his ears and whiskers twitched constantly. "Master Splinter?" he said at last. "Are you all right?"

"Yes…" Splinter responded after a pause. Was it - could it be a flute he seemed to hear playing inside his head? "Yes, I am fine. Please, let us continue the search!"

"I'm worried about Splinter," Leonardo confided to the others. "He's acting strange."

"I've noticed that, too," admitted Donatello.

His voice trailed away as they turned into yet another maze of tunnels. Where was April?

No doubt about it, April was in a tight
spot. There was a gag across her mouth,
and her hands and feet were tightly bound.
Through the gloom, she could make out
some piles of water-logged furniture and
other rubbish. She thought it looked
remarkably like a disused subway she had
reported on, not so long ago.

Feebly she struggled against her bonds.
There were rats scampering everywhere.

"Welcome to my humble abode, Miss
O'Neil!" A sinister, black shadow blocked
out the dim light. "I trust you are
comfortable?"

At first, April saw only his feet. Then she
raised her tired eyes to see a tall stranger
dressed in rags. A rotting bandage wound
around his head revealed two staring eyes
that seemed to burn through the gloom.

With a cruel snigger, he took out a knife to cut April free, hauling her to her feet.

"Who - who are you?" demanded April, pulling down the gag.

"I am his royal rodent majesty, the Rat King! And, these..." he gestured towards the swarms of eager-faced rats, "are my loyal subjects. My simplest wish is their command!"

"Why did you bring me here?" cried April as she was pushed inside a huge cage.

"To keep you from telling those vicious lies about my loyal rat subjects!" was the answer.

The door of the cage slammed shut, leaving April clutching the bars. She saw the Rat King take out something like a flute which he put to his lips, filling the chamber with eerie music...

At once the rats stopped scurrying about and formed into columns, like a miniature army, and began marching on their hind legs!

"Don't you understand?" roared the Rat King in a mad frenzy. "My devoted rodent followers and I are forming a new government in these sewers! And I am their leader!"

April bit her lip, hoping that the Turtles would arrive in mega quick time! Boy, did she need her Turtle-Com. She needed it so badly she could almost hear it bleeping!

As it happened, April *could* hear a Turtle-Com, sounding louder than usual in an empty tunnel. "Leonardo here!" snapped its owner.

"It's Irma! I think I know where April is, and who's got her! It's some nutter called the Rat King!"

"How do you know?" Leonardo was quite impressed - but then he couldn't see Irma flapping the note she'd found pinned on April's dressing room door, reading *"I HAVE APRIL O'NEIL! SIGNED, THE RAT KING!"*

"Oh," she said airily, "call it intuition!"

Sadly, a woman's intuition was no help to April. And being stuck behind bars, with the Rat King looking so smug, was enough to make any lady speak through clenched teeth.

"Just wait till my friends, the Turtles, get here!" she burst out. "They're trained by Splinter, Master of Japanese Martial Arts!"

"Turtles?" scoffed the Rat King. "So, who is their Master? A lizard?"

"If you must know," stormed April, raising her voice above the sniggers, "he's a rat…" As soon as she said it, she clapped a hand over her mouth. But it was too late!

The Rat King's eyes lit up. "A rat, eh?"

"A rat?" April repeated quickly. "Did I say a rat? I meant, he's a bat! No…!" She clutched wildly at her auburn hair. "No, a cat! That's it - a cat, with big fangs and claws!"

"Perfect!" crowed the Rat King, not even listening. "With a Martial Arts Master in my power, I can rule every rodent in the city!"

He turned to his army of adoring rats. "We'll stop those Turtles before they invade our rodent realm! We'll do this by turning their Master against them!"

Once again, the eerie flute-like music began. And, once again, in a nearby tunnel, Donatello could see Master Splinter's eyes glazing over.

"What's wrong?" he cried anxiously.

Confused and dazed, Splinter could only lean against a wall, his pupils dilating.

"I - I feel strange. As if some force is compelling me…"

The Turtles could hear the strange-sounding music now. It was becoming louder and louder. Suddenly, with a mighty splash, the Rat King rose up out of the water, surrounded by his army of rats.

"Halt!" he roared. "You are trespassing!"

"The Rat King…" breathed Donatello. "He's the one who grabbed April!"

The Rat King put the flute to his lips again, filling the chamber with its strange melody.

"That music…" droned Splinter, his eyes glazing once more. "I cannot resist…"

The Rat King laid his flute aside. "Splinter," he said, "from now on, you will obey only me!"

"Yes," agreed Splinter at once, staring straight ahead. "Yes, Your Highness!"

"And my decree is - destroy those Turtles!"

"You command," said Splinter, "I obey!"

Before the Turtles knew what was happening, their Master Splinter had struck a fighting pose and began lashing out with a speed they had never known existed!

"Oooof...!" Donatello crashed into the sewer wall, then slid down into the mucky water.

"Whoooah!" Michaelangelo was twirled around a pipe.

"Oh, no!" groaned Leonardo, dazed and groggy. "Master Splinter may be too much for all of us!"

In a fit of panic, Raphael tried a judo throw on Splinter. But, as always, the Master was too quick, sending him hurtling through the air!

"No, Master!" cried Leonardo desperately, swords ready to defend himself. "Stop!"

But, Splinter was like a madman. He lunged at Leonardo with his stick, hitting the crossed swords!

"Hai!" Leonardo was powerless to stop one

blow after another. "Hai!" Splinter began
hissing in triumph. "Hai! **Hai!**"

"Master Splinter!" Leonardo cried. "Listen
to me! Ignore the Rat King's commands!"

"No, Splinter!" thundered the Rat King. "*I*
am your ruler!"

"There's only one thing to do!" announced
Leonardo. He flung aside his swords and
spread his arms. "I won't defend myself!"

"Now, my loyal subject!" cried the Rat King gleefully, giving Splinter a push. "Finish him!"

"Heeeyaaah!" Splinter threw himself at Leonardo, his hand raised for a deadly karate chop. A second from impact, Leonardo dodged - and Splinter hit the water pipe! The pipe split and water gushed out, drenching the Rat King and his army of rats!

"Master!" shouted Leonardo, as Splinter fell, the spell broken. "You're yourself again!"

"Yes." Only Splinter knew how much the ordeal had exhausted him. "Barely..."

"C'mon," said Raphael, taking him by the arm. "Let's blow this joint!"

"Mondo notion, bud!" agreed Michaelangelo, as they swept away.

"They've escaped!" stormed the Rat King, slamming his fist into the sewer wall. "But, this contest of wills is not over!"

On safer ground, Master Splinter seemed to sense there was more to come, too. The Turtles had never seen him look so tired and worried.

"But, Master," said Leonardo, "your will-power triumphed over the Rat King's! You broke his mind control!"

Master Splinter sighed wearily. "Thank you, Leonardo. But I dare not face him again until my strength returns. That is why you Turtles must continue your search for April - alone!"

"Don't worry, Master!" said Leonardo. "You trained us well! We'll get April back!"

While the Turtles had been searching the sewers, Irma had been busy searching through as many old video tapes of Channel Six news items that she could lay hands on! She seemed to remember April talking about a place that had been particularly rat-infested

Suddenly, she gave a whoop of triumph - there was a shot of a disused subway station...

Almost at the same moment that Irma flicked open April's Turtle-Com to let the Turtles in on her idea, April was using her nail file to open the lock on her cage! She held her breath as a loud click echoed through the stretch of tunnel. She was free!

The Rat King had posted sentries at every exit - all except a broken gate that half-blocked the entrance to another tunnel. April peered inside. It was pitch black, deathly quiet and had a sour smell of dampness. But she knew it was her only chance.

Holding her breath, she stepped into the darkness, blindly looking around for something - anything - to see, to guide her.

A little way ahead she could hear splashing water, and strange-looking shadows began looming towards her.

"Heeyaa! Haaa! Keeyiiii!" A series of wild-sounding cries echoed all around.

"Yeeoww!" April's throat felt so dry and so tight, it was a relief to scream. Then, as she opened her mouth again, a familiar voice called towards her.

"April?" Leonardo sounded surprised, as well as concerned.

"How did you get away?" Donatello asked.

April held up her nail file and gave a big grin. "Let's say it's one for the files!"

She guessed it would not be long before the Rat King found she was missing. And at that very moment, he was coming after her, sniffing the air with his long, hairy nose.

"I smell something... It's a woman's perfume... and the fragrance is getting closer!"

A few more paces - and he leapt out of the shadows, grabbing desperately. "Gotcha!"

"Eeeek!"

It was not April's scream the Rat King heard! But, he did not know that until he stepped back and saw a mound of black hair standing on end, and specs sliding down a shiny nose!

"Who are you?"

"Whoever I am," said Irma, "I'm twenty years older than I was a minute ago!" She pushed the specs back into place. "Hold on! You're that Rat King maniac!"

Without thinking she grabbed out at him, speaking between gritted teeth. "Okay, buster! Where's my pal, April?"

"That's what I'd like to know!" The Rat King sounded quite indignant.

"Well, there's only one way to find out!" Ignoring him, Irma put her hands to her mouth and took a deep breath. "Yoohoo! April!"

"Where are yoooou?" The Rat King joined in, not realising that April and the Turtles could hear him as well as they could hear Irma!

"April," said Leonardo, already racing off, "you stay here!"

"And miss out on a story?" came the reply. "No way!"

"There he is!" cried Leonardo, seeing the black shape a short distance ahead. The Rat King had spotted them, too.

"Now, Turtles!" he boomed, plucking a grenade from his combat gear. "This is the final show-down!"

"Jump, guys!" roared Leonardo, as the missile came hurtling towards them.

He was barely in time. The grenade exploded in the very spot where they had been standing.

April was just congratulating herself on escaping with only a few mud splashes when a dull, whirring sound throbbed through the semi-darkness, followed by a

succession of low groans and dull thuds.
The blurred outlines of Turtles staggered
around, stunned.

Before April could work out what had
happened, a weighted rope swirled around
her, pinning her arms to her sides! The Rat
King had swung his deadly bola weight and
rope, successfully recapturing his victim.

"Bring her back to the palace!" he ordered.

He had not reckoned with Irma! "I'll be
your hostage! Take me, instead!"

The Rat King's tone was distinctly
scornful. "Call me when you've got a
television show!"

"Men!" Irma was really steamed up! "You always go for the redheads!" Angrily, she stamped on the Rat King's foot.

"*Yeow!*" He hopped up and down. "Ouch! Oooh, the hurt! The pain!"

As he hopped, another grenade on his combat belt came adrift. It fell off and splashed into the water, bubbling and hissing ominously.

"Aaaagh!" The Rat King fled in panic, his screams echoing down the long corridor!

"Irma!" shouted Donatello. "Irma, run!"

The words were hardly out of his mouth when there was a terrific explosion. Whole sections of the roof crashed down, missing the Turtles, April and Irma by centimetres!

And when the dust had settled they saw that the fallen brickwork and masonry had totally blocked the tunnel. For anyone - or anything - left inside, there could be no escape.

"So much for the Rat King!" said Donatello.

"For sure!" Michaelangelo nodded grimly. "I seriously doubt we'll see that creepazoid again!"

"I hope you're right!" said Leonardo. "It's a small world, down here in the sewers."

April pushed back a lock of hair from her damp forehead and looked at her watch.

"Well, gang, it's been fun..." She reached out for Irma's arm. "But we've gotta get back to the old rat race!"

As she and Irma left, the Turtles' laughter echoed along the tunnels behind them.